WISH UPON A MOM

BY ADAM BEECHEN   ILLUSTRATED BY TOM LAPADULA

Simon Spotlight/Nickelodeon

New York   London   Toronto   Sydney   Singapore

Butch Hartman

Based on the TV series *The Fairly OddParents*®
created by Butch Hartman as seen on Nickelodeon®

SIMON SPOTLIGHT
An imprint of Simon & Schuster Children's Publishing Division
1230 Avenue of the Americas, New York, New York 10020

SIMON SPOTLIGHT and colophon are
registered trademarks of Simon & Schuster.
Manufactured in the United States of America
First Edition
2 4 6 8 10 9 7 5 3 1
ISBN 0-689-86324-1

"Have a good dinner, dear," Timmy's mother said, absently pouring ketchup into his milk glass as she opened the door for Vicky. "We'll be home after you're in bed. Vicky's here if you need anything."

"But it's Mother's Day," Timmy complained. "I was hoping you'd be home tonight."

"I never get to spend any time with my mom," Timmy said, groaning to Cosmo and Wanda. "I wish she would be with me all the time!"

"Okay, then," Cosmo said as he and Wanda waved their wands. "Your wish is our command!"

"Timmy, I'm home," his mother called out, walking through the door. "I decided I'd rather be with you than at the movies. From now on everywhere you go, I go!"

"That's great, Mom," Timmy replied with a grin.

"I guess we won't be needing you tonight after all, Vicky." Mrs. Turner said,
handing her a few dollars. "In fact, we might not be needing you again for a very
long time!"

Timmy jumped with joy as the door closed on Vicky. "Awesome!" he shouted.

"Looks like this one worked out pretty well," Wanda said with a smile, giving her husband a high five.

"Thanks, you guys," Timmy said. "This was the best wish ever!"

"We're glad you're happy," Cosmo told him.

"Now we're going to spend the rest of Mother's Day and the next few days with Cosmo's mother," Wanda said with a frown. "So much for *us* being happy!"

For the rest of the night Timmy and his mother had a wonderful time together.

They made cookies,

played board games,

and watched a movie.

They even hid behind the couch and surprised
Timmy's dad when he came home late from work.

The next day Timmy's mom drove him to school. Timmy couldn't
remember the last time that had happened—she'd been so busy lately.

"Thanks, Mom," he told her, getting out of the car. "I'll see you after school!"
But to Timmy's surprise his mother got out of the car!
"Don't be silly," she said with a smile. "Everywhere you go, I go! Remember?
Now let's get to class!"

Timmy had never been more embarrassed in his whole life. He could hear his classmates whispering to one another about how he had brought his mother to school. Even worse, when he would get a question wrong his mother would raise her hand and get the answer right!

"Very good, Mrs. Turner," Mr. Crocker said.

Timmy thought he could ditch his mom after school by going to the arcade with his friends. He thought wrong.

Timmy could feel everyone looking at him. His mother was the only adult there. She even beat his high score at Robo-Vampires of the 23rd Century!

That night Mrs. Turner went with Timmy to his Squirrelly Scouts meeting—wearing a Scouts uniform of her own! "Everywhere you go, I go," she reminded him.

"Mom," Timmy whispered, "don't you have your own meeting to go to? Or isn't there something you should be doing at home? Alone?"

"Nonsense, Timmy," she replied with a smile. "The only thing I want to do is be with you!"

"This wish is turning into a nightmare," Timmy muttered to himself the next
morning. "Oh, well. At least it can't get any worse."

That is until his dad announced at breakfast, "I feel like I never see either of you.
From now on everywhere the two of you go, I go!"

"That's wonderful, dear," his mother said. "Now the three of us will always be
together!"

Timmy decided he'd had enough. He had to get in touch with Cosmo and Wanda. But Jorgen Von Strangle stopped him at the gates to Fairy World.

"This is really important, Mr. Von Strangle," Timmy said in his nicest voice. "I need their help. It's about my mother. Didn't you ever have a mother?"

A tear rolled down Jorgen's face. "My dear old Mother Von Strangle," he whispered, and then he waved Timmy into Fairyland. "All right, you can come in. But hurry!"

At Cosmo's mother's house Mama Cosma offered her son another cookie. "I know how much you like them," she told Cosmo, giving Wanda a sideways glance. "And I know you don't get cookies like this at home."

Ding-dong! Jorgen Von Strangle stood in the doorway with Timmy peeking out from behind him.

"I am sorry to interrupt your special visit with your mother," Jorgen said. "But there is a fairy emergency." He waved sweetly at Mama Cosma. "Hello. So sorry."

Wanda excitedly grabbed her husband's hand. "Too bad we can't stay," she said quickly. "But you heard him. There's an emergency! Come on, honey!"

"I decided I like being with my mom, just not every minute of every day! I wish everything would be back to normal," Timmy told Cosmo and Wanda. POOF!

"Timmy," his mother said, suddenly walking in, "I just remembered I have a meeting, and so does your father. We should be home in time to kiss you good night, all right?"

"That's great, Mom," Timmy answered with a smile. "Have a really, really, really good meeting!"

Just then Vicky stepped into the room.

"We're leaving now," Mrs. Turner said. "Have fun with Vicky, sweetie!"

Timmy rushed across the room. "Hi, Vicky," he said, hugging her legs. "I can't believe I'm going to say this, but I'm actually happy to see you."